WHAT IS
SPIRITUALITY?

By Rev Kate Kay

Rev Kate Kay

INTRODUCTION:

There are so many ways the word is used today, both religious and non-religious; spiritual, spiritualism, spiritualist, spiritual gift, full of the spirit (either the Holy Spirit or full of alcohol), born of the spirit, spirit based, the Holy Spirit, the theology of spirituality, the spirit of our fathers etc......

Talking to people some have a vague idea what it means, some think it refers to those who are ordained or those who've taken vows, others have no real idea, but it may be something to avoid. Having been researching, and found a large amount of different definitions on line and in books I can understand why people are confused about the word and suspicious of its meaning. I have used chapter one as a place to look at a portion of these definition and provide ones which will be focused on in the other chapters.

Although this is not meant as a form of Bible study, the questions at the end of the chapters were there for further thought, could be used as a study. Each chapter follows on from each other, but equally they can be used or read out of order if there is something in particular you're looking information on.

WHERE DO I BEGIN?

I thought it would be best to begin by looking for a definition of spirituality, but that ended up being a larger task than I realised. Both the internet and books came up with so many varied definitions I decided to share some of them with you, instead of looking for one definition.

Google defines spirituality as:

> "The quality of being concerned with the human spirit or soul as opposed to material or physical things." (Dictionary)

> "The meaning of spirituality has developed and expanded overtime, and various connotations can be found alongside each other." (Wikipedia)

> "In general it includes a sense of correction of something bigger than ourselves and it typically involves a search for meaning in

life." (takingcharge.chs.com)

All of these are vague enough to cover both secular and religious situations in life, without them appearing overly religious. The following definitions are from religious books, although they all focus on different points and thoughts.

Discerning your spirituality – J Hinton.

> "Spirituality is a word that describes the part of ourselves that lies within, that influences our decisions and the course of our lives – hidden, yet extremely powerful." [1]

> "Everyone has spirituality, but not every person nourishes that part of their being. It is here to in the deepest part of our being that we can come to know God, who is Spirit." [2]

> "Sometimes the word 'Spirituality' is used in only a limited sense. It's used to describe a person's relationship to God, but it is more than this – it is about the way we relate to the whole of our life." [3]

Signposts to Spirituality – T Hudson.

> "Spirituality is a slippery word. Some are suspicious of its presence. For when daily lives revolve around frantic timetables of preparing breakfast, getting children to school on time, holding down a stressful eight to five job, paying monthly accounts and cleaning the house, the word sounds something strange and im-

practical. It suggests another world of inactivity, passivity and uninterrupted silence."[4]

Spirituality and Pastoral care – K Leech.

"True spirituality involves a dimension of listening, of abandonment, of silent brooding, features which are conspicuously absent in most fundamental worship and life." [5]

Spirituality and Theology – Sheldrake.

"Spirituality is all-embracing and encompassing all aspects of living, spirituality may include behaviours and the attitude that underlies it. In that sparse spirituality overlaps with ethics, but cannot be reduced to it." [6]

Beyond Boundaries – J Robinson.

"So what is spirituality? We can only indicate. It is about life in the Spirit. It is too big to be defined, as it belongs to the inner world of being. Certainly it is relationship and finding inspiration and faith in daily living. It is about kindness, and our concern for a compassionate society, for the natural world of which we are part, for peace and justice and ethos of living appropriate for our time." [7]

The Spiritual Workbook – Runcorn.

"If vocation is about loving God and allowing him to love us, then Spirituality is about how we live that love in our daily lives." [8]

The Study of Spirituality – ed. Jon, Wainright, Yarweald.

> "What then is spirituality.......It is by no means to be confused with theology which is chiefly an elaboration of concepts. It is a life. All human existence has a spiritual aspect....Although the notion of spirituality is definitely a Christian notion, it be no means limits its attention to the Catholic world or the Christian world. To exhibit the spirituality of human reality is to embrace this reality to its full extent, and such a quest does not just interest a few specialists." [9]

> "It is difficult to find any one characteristic which marks Anglican Spirituality as a whole during the twentieth century. During this time the Anglican spiritual tradition has been open to influences from many quarters and has shown a remarkable capacity to assimilate material of various kinds. Perhaps it is this very openness to others which should be seen as the dominant feature of this period." [10]

Wisdom Distilled from the Daily – J Chittester

> "Spirituality is more than churchgoing. It is possible to go to Church and never develop a spirituality at all." [11]

There is a lot of information in each of these quotes, and there is a variety of explanations of how different people understand Spirituality. There does seem to be a theme running through the majority of them concerning; God, The Holy Spirit, the creation, us, love, our lives, an inner life.

Maybe now would be a good time to re-read some of these definitions and then consider:

> Are there any definitions which really speak to us?
>
> How do they relate to where I am now?
>
> How do they relate to who I am?
>
> How do they relate to my vision of God?

Now might also be a good time to look more closely at our view of God. Has or view of God changed during our lives or is it still basically the same?

Get a piece of paper and write God in the middle, then write down all the words which you feel describes God, and also which describe your relationship to Him and His relationship to you.

There are two definitions which struck a chord with me; the one by Robinson, which I felt brought out some of the mystery of God and the fact that no matter how much we learn or come near God there will always be more for us to discover. The second was by Runcorn, partially I suppose because I spent a while researching the topic of vocation and his definition seems to bring both words together and provides a description of a Christian's life.

You will have seen in the above quotes that people feel it's not easy to define spirituality or to give an explanation of how it has changed as Christianity has developed over the centuries, but having taken all that into view the aim of the next few chapters is to look at ways we can begin to draw closer to God, and begin to understand a little of what Spirituality may mean in our lives.

To this end we will be looking at; the Bible, pray, Church, theology, and some history of Christianity.

> Love your body.
>
> You are not a body,
>
> Not a no-body
>
> Not just any-body
>
> But some-body.
>
> The body is the dwelling place
>
> Of the whole making Spirit.
>
> (Prayers at Night by J. Cotter, Pg 61.)

DO I NEED TO READ THE BIBLE?

If we begin with the concept that Spirituality is about you and God, (which was in our previous chapter) then the answer is obviously 'Yes', you need to read the Bible. How else can you learn about God, His love, His Son, His forgiveness and many other things as well? But you don't need to read it from cover to cover like you would any other reading books. The Bible is a book you need to read slowly, think, listen and pray, just as you wouldn't eat a roast meal in one bite, so the Bible is read bit at a time so you can be fed by God.

William Temple wrote, "If people live with a wrong view of God, the more religious they become the worse the consequences will be and eventually it would be for better for them to be atheists."[12]

This is why we ended the last chapter by thinking about God, more specifically how we think about or visual God. Your understanding has been formed over many years through your parent's views, through Church or Sunday School, through RE lessons at school, what you see and hear from others and from where you grew up or live now. Although you may never have specifically talked about God with these people, the information will be there in your head stored away, possible affecting your view of God and Church without even realising it or knowing why you feel that way.

Dalles Willard points out, "We live at the mercy of our ideas, we would be wise to reflect carefully upon those that we have heard about God." [13]

The way we come to know God and to compare our thoughts is to read the Bible. So as we look more at Bible passages have to hand your piece of paper, so you can compare your thoughts with those in the Bible. Sometimes when I look back on thoughts about God, I can almost hear or see the person who said what I remembered.

If we start with Genesis chapter one verse one, we can see that God is not singular as the Word and the Spirit were both present at creation.

> "In the beginning God created the heavens and the earth. The earth was without form or void and darkness was upon the face of the deep; and the Spirit of God was moving over the face of the waters. (Gen 1:1-2)

> "Then God said, 'Let us make man in our image,

after our likeness'....... So God created in His own image, in the image of God He created them, male and female He created them." (Gen 1:26 – 27)

Kenneth Leech writes, "Biblical Spirituality is social Spirituality. It is a Spirituality of the kingdom of God, of a pilgrim people, of the Body of Christ."[14]

The social aspect is seen in both the Old Testament and the New Testament. God calls His people, leads them to the Promised Land; provides the Ten Commandments so they know how to live and appoints prophets to speak to His people, particularly when things aren't going well.

Then in the New Testament He sends Jesus to take upon Himself all the sins of the world, so that His creation can be in relationship with Him. His greatest desire is to share His love with us and for us to love Him, and ultimately share His love with those people around us, and those we meet every day.

Today society seems to relate to a more individual spirituality with an emphasis on personal growth and enlightenment, and a need to be better than your neighbour rather than relating to them. Leech feels that this is more like classic Gnosticism with a concern for self-knowledge and illumination rather than the Biblical tradition. This is quite different from the New Testament and particularly different to the teaching of St. Paul. [15]

In Roman's Paul writes about the need to encourage each other and help with the building up of the Body of Christ, (Rom 1:12, 12:5, 14:9) again in the first letter to Corinthians there is mention of the body of Christ and the need to work together and help each other to grow and develop as Christians. (1 Cor 10:17, 12:7, 12:12, 14:12) This is the main message in the majority of his epistles and it is something which people feel is missing from some of our Churches. If you go to a bookshop you will find rows of self-help books, mindfulness books, colouring books, as well as a few books from religious authors, but the majority of them talk about yourself, your life, your growth and development, and very little about relating to God or neighbour.

"Christian spirituality is about a process of formation, a process in which we are formed by and in Christ." (Phil 2:6)

Runcorn write, "Christian Spirituality is a way of service, not self-fulfilment…..Intercession lies at the heart of Christian prayer…..The centre of Christian living and praying is not about what we seek for ourselves. It is concerned with God's glory and with the needs of others." [16]

He quotes Michael Ramsay as saying, "It is standing before God with the people on your heart." [17]

If you look up 'intercede', it is about being a 'go between', so the Bible is calling us to stand between those in need and God, as part of our spiritual life. Which means that intercession/prayer is not so much about what or who we are praying for but where we are in our relationship with God.

Some of you may know the song by Dan Schute;

> "Here I am Lord, is it I Lord,
>
> I have heard you calling in the night?
>
> I will go Lord, if you lead me,
>
> I will hold your people in my heart."

This fits well with the social aspect of Christianity which we are called to live.

So how do we cope with a world that values independence, self-growth, self-reliance and self-realization, and a Church which is calling us to grow and mature as a member of the Body of Christ where the self is seen in relationship with God and with our neighbour? Somehow our spirituality needs to build a bridge between a society of individuals and a Church working together as one in God. The only way we can achieve this is by deepening our relationship with God.

As Kenneth Leech says, "To be a Christian is to be part of an organism, a new community, the extension of the Incarnation." [18]

There is a need to bring the Bible out of the Church and home with us so we can read it, not in a study type way, but meditate upon the words and actions of Jesus, the disciples, Paul and the prophets. It's very difficult to take something into your life and let it help you to grow if you are only analysing it, you need to pray it, inwardly digest it, allow it to become one with you and through this become one with God Father, Son and Holy Spirit.

Go through Paul's letters and read them slowly, focusing on what he is teaching the new and older Christians in the different towns. Then ask yourself what you can learn along with these people about being Christians but also about being a community according to Paul. Some of these people Paul are writing to may have seen Jesus, some may not have, but they are all eager to listen and learn about Jesus' death, resurrection and ascension, and how this relates to their lives as a person, as a church and as a community.

In 1 Peter 2:5 we are called to be a royal priesthood; "And like living stones be yourselves built into a spiritual house, to be a holy priesthood, to offer spiritual sacrifices acceptable to God." In chapter 9 he continues, "But you are a chosen race, a royal priesthood, a holy nation, God's own people, that you may declare the deeds of Him who called you out of darkness into His marvellous light."

After Jesus returned to His Father many things happened, the disciples went out to teach and baptize new Christians, many new books were written, some not quite following the teaching of Christ, other by the Church Fathers, often refuting the way people were teaching about Jesus, often teaching the words which had come down from the disciples.

Over these years the Bible was put together into basically what we have now, and extra books were added into other groups along with new writings. The creed was put together basically as an attempt to state what we do believe and also against some of the sects and there teaching. The Church also became linked with the state instead of the sundry other gods which used to be linked with it.

There were also people who felt called out from society to pray and be with God. These first sets of people tried many different ways of living, but the main three forms were:

> In Lower Egypt – hermits

> In Upper Egypt – monks and nuns in communities.

> In Nitria and Sectis – solitaries living in groups of three or four. (A master and disciples)

These were called the Desert Fathers/Mothers; mostly they were simple folks, peasants from around the Nile area. "Often, the first thing that struck those who heard about the Desert Fathers was the negative aspects of their lives." [19] The majority of these were illiterate and there saying were passed down. Reading about these people gave you a different view on life, as they focuses not on what they lacked but on what they had. They went against the world's view about needs for property and goods, for sex and not to accept direction for another, (It almost sound a little like today's society in some places.)

"It was because of this positive desire for the kingdom of Heavens which came to dominate their lives that they went without things......They were learning to listen to something more interesting than the talk of man, that is, the Word of God." [20]

In the Old Testament the desert was a place to go out and meet God, to hear His word, which may be missed in the bustle of everyday life. In the New Testament the desert was the place where the Spirit led/sent/forced Jesus after His Baptism.

As a passing thought, the Greek word used to describe the dove at Jesus' Baptism, is not the gentle white dove we see in so many pictures. The word refers to a rock dove which lives in very inhospitable places like the rocky crags found out in the desert. This is the dove that challenges us, reshapes us, and reorders our lives to lead us in a way for which we have no control. This is what is leading us and our Church into a God given future.

So each of us is being called by the Spirit into the desert, not in reality, but the desert within, we will all be tempted as Jesus was and we will be pruned by God into the person He created us to be. This is where we will be transformed and where our eyes will be opened and our egos will be put to one side so that God's love will be the centre of our lives.

❖ In essence we are the person God made us, but the image has been marred by sin and by many outside influences as we grew up.

❖   Have you felt the Holy Spirit at work in your life? If you look back can you see places where God was at work in your life?

Christ be with me, Christ within me,
Christ behind me, Christ before me.
Christ beside me, Christ to win me,
Christ to comfort and restore me,
Christ beneath me, Christ above me,
Christ in quiet, Christ in danger,
Christ in hearts of all who love me,
Christ in mouth of friend and stranger.
(A section of St. Patricks Breastplate. [21])

DO I NEED TO
GO TO CHURCH
OR PRAY?

"**E**ach Church, and probably each theologian within each Church, would probably produce a different theology of Spirituality." [22]

The whole question of theology is going to be discussed in the next chapter, for now we need to think about how we understand spirituality in relation to the liturgy of the Church and in relation to prayer. Taking the statement above, why is it that, every person we meet and every book we read has a different interpretation of spirituality and prayer? The difference wasn't always there, if you look back to the disciples they were following Jesus, but since then things have changed and grown and in this process things began to vary in different regions, with different teachers, with different translations of the Bible, with different emphasis being placed on different parts of Jesus' ministry and so on. In the twelfth century theology became intellectual and moved from monastery to big cities for the Western Church, but not for the Eastern Church. So with theology and spirituality separated spirituality became an internal, often individual, part of life.

"Medieval Spirituality (in as far as generalizations are possible) was essentially public, communal and 'ecclesial' in nature and focused in the liturgy of the Church, the Bible and the cults of saints. The effects of the reformation, and its challenges to the divine authority of human institutions and traditions, was to give considerable impetus to a more privatized and internalized Spirituality." [23]

So we have theology being for study and intellectual people, spirituality for the inward growth of people, the monasteries and the Eastern Church still trying to unite both, and the people in the pews left to try and work things out for themselves.

In the twentieth century things began to change:

➢ In 1904 there were the beginnings of the Pentecostal Church.

➢ In the 1960's the Charismatic movement began to provide a fresh approach to worship, sharing the ministry across the whole community and beginning the ministry of healing.

➢ There was also influence from the Taize community, Vatican II and Lambeth 1968.

21

➢ Retreats and spiritual direction was also becoming popular and essential for growth.

"An individual's spiritual development means growth towards a fuller union with God through prayer and a growing conformity to God's call in life."[24]

Times were beginning to change; liturgy and prayer were being influenced by the Holy Spirit, which gave a new framework that was bringing new life to people and Churches. More Churches began looking at the Bible and the spiritual gifts which were described in the New Testament, and the idea of the Church being a family, bring a community, being the Body of Christ, began to influence liturgy so it moved from people sitting and priest doing everything, to a shared liturgy belonging to the community of the Church.

This movement forward has continued and moved into the twenty-first century, with new forms of liturgy, more modern words for liturgy and for hymns and a feeling for many that they are the Church of God. (There still are those Churches for whom this movement forward has been painful and difficult.)

"Prayer is at the heart of all religion, but for many Christian's prayer has become something of an embarrassment." [25]

We all feel safe praying within the liturgy as there is a set form of words, or a plan to follow, (ie. praying for the world, the church, the sick the dead). The question then is, should we pray at home or is once a week enough? Why do we find praying at Church easy; because there is a set of word, at home is more difficult as we haven't got a set of words, unless we use the offices. When you look at books in a book-shop or library there are so many different books, so many different ways of going about things, and then there's those big words – contemplation, medita-tion, mysticism, silence – (I can hear you thinking... 'those surely are for monks or nuns',) plus people talk about retreats, solitude, and so many other things, how can you decide which is right for you or at least which to begin with. So how can we know where to begin?

"Spiritual maturity does not occur as a result of the accumulation of skills and techniques.... but as a re-sult of the reality of the Word of God challenging, piercing, and shaping us: the reality of the encoun-ter with ourselves, with God and with the depths in other people through silence and darkness." [26] The problem is that talking about deserts, tests and darkness can come across as discouraging, rather than encouraging. So we need to start from where we are.

One of the quotes from Chapter one was, "If voca-tion is about loving God and allowing Him to love you, then spirituality is about how we live that love out in our lives." [8]

So beginning where we are means thinking about spirituality as our relationship with God, the total sum of which is for Him to love us, we love Him and then share that love with our neighbours.

I hear you asking, so where does prayer fit in?

Think about your relationships with friends and family, how do you keep these flourishing, how do you deepen some of your friendships? By keeping in contact with them, by phone, letter, text, face time, skype, etc, God is exactly the same except instead of meeting Him on skype or texting Him we pray. As we grow as Christians we begin to realize that the talking isn't that important as listening to Him. Any good relationship needs to include both talk and listening, so does our relationship with God. We need to listen, to allow Him to share His love with us, to rest in His arms and learn from Him about the person He created us to be. Jesus is our example, after a busy day ministering the Bible tells us that He would go off somewhere quiet to pray and be with God.

Frank Lubeck says, "Explorers in the realm of the Spirit are like Columbus when he landed on a new continent and did not know what lay beyond. We have probably only just reached the beach heads in our prayers. A vast continent lies before us to be explored, conquered and cultivated. Nothing is as thrilling as discovery. Every Christian can and should join in the highest of all adventures in the most wonderful of all worlds, the world of the Spirit." [27]

Prayer shouldn't be something we feel over-whelmed by, instead we should feel joy at being able to spend time with, to learn our path in life from, and discover how great God's love is for us. As we grow we can find many new things, ways to share in God's love, ways to hear Him speak to us; it should be as Frank Lubeck describes a new and exciting journey.

Where do we begin though? Simply by setting aside a few minutes each day to ask God to bless the day ahead, or by reflecting in the evening about what happened during the day.

"Prayer is about finding the most suitable rhythm to enable one to develop a meaningful, vibrant relationship with the living God. He has chosen to make us all different from one another. Each of us must find the prayer pattern that is most suited to foster the development of our relationship with the creator God. He did not make us to be clones of one another."[28]

There are booklets you can get which provide a reading, reflection and prayer for each day or you may prefer to read a chapter from one of the Gospels and reflecting on it. Look at what Jesus does and says; reflect on how this would have affected you if He was speaking to you, and ask God to help you understand further.

There are also books looking at various saints that provide a prayer or short story about their life. It really doesn't matter what it is, the important part is beginning to spend time with God, and in a place you feel comfortable.

"Pray as you can, don't try to pray as you can't." [29] If people suggest books or ways to pray thank them, try it, but don't panic if they don't work for you.

You need to find your own way as we are all individuals. "Prayer is essentially….a love affair with God, not skills or techniques or ways of prayer, but the most direct, open approach of each one of us as a person to God our creator, redeemer and sanctifier…..We seek God Himself, not thoughts about Him, but about ourselves in relationship with Him."[30]

Having looked at the present day, for the rest of this chapter I want to go back a few centuries and look at different ways people and communities approach spirituality prior to the twelfth Century.

We will begin with Celtic Spirituality. This is primarily presented down the ages by oral tradition, in the form of prayers, poetry, storytelling and songs. It is a spirituality which makes use of rich imagination, which is shaped by their earthy experiences. There is a strong emphasis on the Trinity in their prayers, which are not just spoken, but lived out in their daily lives. Before Christianity they had a very vivid sense of what was scared in their lives and in the world around them.

> "The Grace of God be with you,
> The Grace of Christ be with you,
> The Grace of the Spirit be with you,
> And with your children,
> For an hour, forever, for eternity." [31]

This is a prayer pattern typical of Celtic Spirituality, particularly for early morning and late night devotion and in blessings.

One who brought Christianity to some of the Celts

was St Patrick. After beginning life as a slave in Ireland, from which he escaped, a year later he heard "The voice of those who were by the Wood of Voclat which is near the Western sea calling, 'Holy boy we are asking you to come and walk among us again'." [32] Early in his "Confessions" he wrote a 'Rule of Faith' (conf 4), which was in Latin, far better than his own, so it was thought that this was from the Faith of the British Churches. In Confession 14 Patrick writes, "'I must teach from the rule of faith of the Trinity', which is, in part, his way of interpreting Christs call to mission. Winning the Irish from paganism and superstition was, indeed, Patrick's life work." [33]

Patrick had a simple faith. He believed that God, the Holy Trinity would supply all his needs. His knowledge of the Bible was very good and he drew on this for both his teaching and his writing. "From his time in captivity he based his life on prayer. It was through prayer that he discovered God's will and gained the strength to do it." [34]

There are three others whose spirituality would be good to look at, Augustine of Hippo, Anselm of Canterbury and Benedict of Nursa.

"Much, specifically Western Christian spirituality is indebted to Augustine. The twelfth century mystics Bernard and Richard of St Victor were both Augustinian Canons, later medieval mystics such as St Teresa and the author of 'The Cloud of Unknowing' were deeply influenced by Augustinian, and Martin Luther was an Augustinian monk." [35]

Because friendship was so important to Augustine, when he was converted he decided the easiest way to follow God was as part of a community. So in 388 he set up a community with his friend. Then in 395 when he became Bishop of Hippo he set up a monastery for clerics in the Bishop's house in Hippo.

During his time mysticism took shape as the highest form of the spiritual life. His understanding was that when one loves God it makes the mystical experience a relationship between persons. Within his communities the love of God and the love of your neighbour were the basis of life. Through prayer, offices, work and fellowship they became one with each other and in turn one with the Trinitarian God.

In 529 St Benedict founded a monastery in Montecassio. Benedict created a rule for the monasteries he started, which he wrote in 529AD; it consists of a prologue and seventy-three chapters. It is called a rule, but not in the way we understand a rule. "Regula, the word now translated to mean rule, in the ancient sense meant guidepost or railing, something to hang onto in the dark, something that leads in a given direction, something that points out the road, something that gives us support." [36] It provided teaching for the monks about living their daily lives and also about virtues of humility, silence and obedience. It also includes information about common prayer, meditative reading, manual work, clothing, sleeping arrangements, food and drink, care of the sick, finding new members, looking after guests and journeys away from the monastery, plus many more things. There are many points which can be seen as core values for Benedictine Spirituality, but the main ones would be moderation in all things, dignity of work, listening, common good, stewardship and justice. "Benedictine spirituality is more about living life well, than about keeping the law perfectly." [37]

Anselm was a Benedictine monk and quite a prolific writer. "He shared his was of prayer by sending copies of his own prayers to certain people and by giving some guidance on how to use them." [38] The rule of St Benedict was very obvious in his prayers and in his other writings.

"God of truth
I ask that I may receive
So that my joy may be full.
Meanwhile, let my mind meditate on it
Let my tongue speak of it,
Let my heart love it,
Let my mouth preach on it,
Let my soul hunger for it,
My flesh thirst for it,
And my whole being desire it,
Until I enter into the joy of my Lord,
Who is God, one and triune, blessed for ever.
Amen.

(From 'Proslogian', in 'Prayers and Meditations of St Anselm' trans. into modern English by St Benedicta Ward SLG, pp226-7.) [39]

Despite the differences in years, locations and communities, two things remain central to these three, Love of God and Prayer.

There is a lot of use in today's world of labels, putting things in boxes so they are easier for people to control. Neither the love of God or prayer are things which can easily put into a box, nor are things like contemplation, meditation, mysticism or other words we read about in books. These words are all about our relationship with God, and neither God nor relationships are easily boxed, and if you do put them in a box you are greatly limiting them in your life. How can you, "Be still and knows that I am God"[40] if God and prayer are each in their own little box? How can you grow and develop as a Christian if there are four solid walls around God and your faith?

Silence is one thing many people try to avoid, using business, work, children and many other things to explain why it is just not possible to have silence. Silence in the Orthodox religion is 'Hesychia', also called prayer of the heart. It is not just about there being no noise around us; it is about something which happens inside us, where we are vigilant and attentive to the word of God. You may ask, 'Why silence?' The answer is simple, yes, God wants to hear your concerns for creation, world and friends but He also wants to talk to you. He knows all our thoughts and needs before we even ask them, what He truly wants is to spend time with you, to help you know yourself as He made you.

"If we are truly to know ourselves, to accept ourselves, without fear of the darkness and turmoil within us, we need to cultivate the gift of silence."[41] God made us and knows us, but as we grow things happen and part of us can be changed, feeling, pains, worries, fears are often hidden away and it is all covered up by a mask called, 'I'm fine thank you.' We each wear it every day as we go to school, to work or out shopping, sometimes loving God and our neighbour is a whole lot easier than loving ourselves, so we hide behind our mask. But we are kidding ourselves, how can we truly love our neighbours who were made by God and not love ourselves, who are also made by God. You can't love God fully if you pick and choose which parts of His creation you want to love.

All God asks of us, is that we allow Him to love us, and in turn we love Him and then share His love with others. If we can trust Him enough to accept His love He will heal our wounds, forgive our sins, and make us back into a whole person. The person He created us to be. But this can be very difficult task after so many years of hiding things deep below. Our bodies don't help us either, every time we sit quietly to meet with God, thoughts appear, an itch, then the phone rings, or the doorbell goes and we just never get back to God. Some days the more you try, the worse your mind seems to fight against you. We need to be honest with God, get Him to help us maybe two or three minutes at a time. He's been waiting all through our lives, a few more days as we gradually find time, find peace, and find courage to face things, isn't going to upset Him. I find focusing on my breathing helps, others find music helps, or looking at an icon or a candle. If thoughts come, acknowledge them and put them to one side and refocus, but don't become frustrated or angry with yourself. The walls you have put up through your life around the inner you will take time to pull down. God knows all your difficulties and always accepts what you are able to give each day.

➢   What are some of the wounds in your heart that make it hard for you to love yourself?
➢   How would you characterise your love of God?

"Tis from my mouth that my prayer I say,
Tis from my heart that my prayer I pray,
Tis before thee that my prayer I lay.
Top thyself, O healing hand I call,
O thou Son of God who save us all."[42]
(Pg. 103, Poems of the Western Highlands.)

DO I NEED TO GO TO COLLEGE?

"Our attempts to talk about the Christian doctrines of God cannot be separated from personal faith and spiritual experience."[43]

But this is not what happened. As we said in chapter three, during the twelfth century scholars began to understand that theology was intellectual and really didn't belong to the monasteries. So it was all moved into centres of learning (known now as Universities) in the larger towns. Prior to this spirituality was sometimes called ascetical and mystical theology.

When Thomas Aquinas wrote his, 'Summa Theologica' he divided his book into separate sections which also added to the divisions and development of the theological disciplines, and spirituality moved further away.

In the early Church a "Theologian was one who contemplated the mystery of the Incarnation and possessed an experience of faith." [44] This continued with pastoral theory and practise, all based around the Bible, and all interpretations of the Bible were based on deepening Christian life.

Who God is and how we relate to Him are questions which cannot solely be left to the intellect, they are questions that are based in Christian faith and need to be lived out each and every day as well as studying them. To fully understand the theology of God, the Incarnation, the Trinity and the death and resurrection of Christ you need to base your learning within your own life and how you live it. Theology and spirituality need to be linked and worked through in the context of the Church and within each and every Christian.

Sheldrake says, "A theology that is alive is always grounded in spiritual experience. Theology needs to be lived just as much as it is studied." [45] He continues, "Spirituality that is individualistic in tone fails to reflect the communion of equal relationship that is in the God-in-Trinity." [46]

The Trinity, Incarnation, Christology, eschatology etc all need to be understood not just by reading, or by individual thoughts and prayers, they need to have their context within the Christian people who are part of the body of Christ.

What would be the point of a trainee chef spending four years studying books, writing essays and passing exams, and then being placed in a professional kitchen and expected to fit in and get on?

So, where does this leave us? Desperately buying books, going on courses or going to university or college to learn more so we can put it into practise in our lives? Maybe reading the Bible, going to Church, listening, watching, asking questions, and then putting all that into practise. I can't tell you what the answer is for you, as you will need to be the judge of what is going to help you, but whether you do all the above or none of it, as a Christian the call to prayer, listening and to be silent needs to be our strongest calling alongside anything else we choose to do.

Having moved all the intellectual studies out of the monasteries what happened in the monasteries, did the monks go and teach in these new centres of learning or did they find other professors to take their place? Quite possibly, but the monasteries continued with their lives of prayer, study and work. It is the monasteries which we now turn to for more information on spirituality and how people were living it out in their daily lives.

Julian of Norwich was one of these people, although little is really known about her life, we assume she was Benedictine as her cell was under the control of Carrow Abbey. "About 600 years ago she told her readers to forget her and look to Christ." [47]

The lives of anchorites and anchoress's were highly regarded by their fellow Christians, it was a discipline and austere life, but they were sort after as spiritual guides and counsel by those living nearby and often those far away as well.

What we know of her life is primarily about her 'showings'.

"At the time of her revelations she was sick to the point of death. Having received the last rites, her parish priest came to her early on the morning of May 8th. He brought a cross and asked her to set her gaze upon it. Though reluctant at first to do so, she tells us, since she had composed herself to death, but she obeyed. After a short period in which she felt herself to be dying, her pain suddenly left her and a series of wonderful 'showings', as she calls then, began. During the next twelve or so hours fifteen revelations of God's love, centring on the cross of the Lord were given to her. Then followed a gap of some hours during which she was terribly afflicted by evil, and then in the early hours of Monday morning the sixteenth and final revelation came."[48]

She spent the next twenty years contemplating them and during this time God gave her a deeper understanding which she in turn wrote out for others to read.

"The subject is love, God's love for human kind shown forth particularly in the cross of our Lord Jesus, and the responsive love in men towards His maker, keeper and lover."[49]

"Would you know the Lord's meaning? Know it well: love was His meaning. Who revealed it to you? Love. What did He reveal to you? Love. Why does He reveal it to you? For love……. I saw very certainly that before God made us He loved us, which love was never abated and never shall be."[50]

Now we move onto Francis, who laid great stress on Christ's passion and death and also on the poverty of Christ.

"Both Clare and Francis sought to put God, as revealed in the poverty of Christ, at the heart of their lives, living simply as brothers and sisters to all that exists." [51]

Their lives were based on simplicity and intensity, with poverty as the answer to the world's greed and materialism. They had an understanding of the glory that is ours in Christ, which came through His cross. Their rule was based around Matt 10:59 and Luke 9:23.

Another community which looked for simplicity in life was the Carmelites. The first brother were seeking a deeper way of following Jesus, so they went to Christ's birth place and lived out the gospel call to simplicity as pilgrims. The word was always central and they tried to live a prophetic life of the word. They lived as hermits, gathering for Mass, reflecting on the scriptures and urged on by love.

The Dominicans also believed in the centrality of the Word, but they lay great emphasis on clarity or reason, precise doctrine and the sanctity of the Mass.

Two books with uncertain authors are the 'Imitation of Christ' and 'The Cloud of Unknowing'.

The 'Imitation of Christ' was originally as four books, so the title is a little misleading as it is the title of the first of the four books, not the whole set. It is thought to be written by Thomas a Kempis who was an Augustinian monk. He was said to be a man of meditation and imitations and the book is a mirror of his inner life and some think an autobiography. By his contemporaries he was known for intellectual attainments, scholarly acquisitions and devout habits. The books are as follows:

➢ Book 1 is about material that applies most directly to the monastic way of life.

➢ Book 2 speaks of a closer friendship with Jesus and how humble, loving submission brings peace.

➢ Book 3 talks of the fruits of close relationships and the love and joy it brings.

➢ Book 4 is about preparation for the Holy Communion and the growth in maturity in the spiritual life.

The different books show the development in a Christian life, as well as showing how a relationship with God is available to all who are willing to find time in their busy days and are willing to face the truth about themselves and who they are.

The 'Cloud of Unknowing' was written around the same period and is thought to have been written by a Cistercian hermit or a Carthusian priest. The writing suggests the author was a skilled theologian and a wise director of souls. There are two other works which have been attributed to the same author.

The book makes the most emphatic distinction between the physical and the spiritual, and followed the negative way of contemplation. The author claims Dionysius as the chief inspiration for his method and aims to destroy the bonds which chain the individual to the world.

"Dionysius describes kataphatic or affirmative way to the divine as the 'way of speech': that we can come to some understanding of the transcendent by attributing all the perfections of the created order to God as its sources. In this sense we can say 'God is love', 'God is beauty', 'God is good'. The apophatic or negative way stresses God's absolute transcendence and unknowability in such a way that we cannot say anything about the divine essence because God is so totally beyond being." [52]

One other I would like to touch on briefly is St Ignatius of Loyola. Ignatius was a soldier initially, but after being injured he was left convalescing with two books to read, the first being "The Life of Christ", and the other "Lives of Saints". After months of reading these books his dreams of knights and glorious battles, changed to fighting for God and a better understanding of his life and his new purpose for life.

He founded the Jesuit order in 1536 and the exercise he had written became a training program for the monks. "According to what Ignatius wrote at the end of the spiritual exercises, the spiritual experience illustrated the generosity of God, who freely shares rays of Himself – graces, virtue and created gifts. Ignatius came to understand this generosity as an important part of the material intimacy that we desire – the sharing of good and self." [53]

Over the years the exercises have been used by many monks and nuns, but now increasingly more lay people are also using them. They are seen by many as a distinctive way to learn about spirituality and life in the world. The biggest problem of course is that most lay people can't get thirty days off to spend with a director working through the exercise.

If you put Ignatius' exercises into google you come up with some very useful pages about how you can do the exercises over a longer time span or in a simpler form. There you will also find videos and many pages to help you understand your ways through the tasks set for each day. The Ignatian Adventure is the right length to use for a Lentern study; with readings to complete each day, along with prayers and meditations for your prayer time. One of the useful things is called the 'Examen' which is where we reflect on finding God in everything around us and everything we experience. Seeing God in the world around us and the people we met, and the places we visit. God is everywhere, but so often we aren't aware of His presence. Walking through the day with God, in the evening before we sleep, is a good way to realise those times during the day when we could have done more, or done things differently, or just been aware that God is in that person. How we greet people, relate to them, once we realise that they are a creation of God's and He dwells in them as He does in us.

Maggie Ross says, "You cannot tell a 20 year old what it feels like to be 40....even if they have read everything on 40 year olds. They lack the tangible wealth of 'experience of life."

The same is true of the journey to God..... while a certain generic spirituality – for example Camelite or Ignatian – may be useful for people whose journeys follow certain landmarks of that particular way, it is not the only way , it is not the universal way." [54]

Ruth Folke agrees with this when she says, "We all do well to remember that differences are not deficiencies." [55]

Ross also thinks, "If reflecting on our spiritual exercise made us spiritual, or holiness, holy....it seems equally absurd to insist on progress or stages. There is a sense of movement and change, a sense of transition." [56]

So, no matter how much you read in this book or in others, no matter how often you read about the lives of the saints, or read about different communities Rules, your experience is your experience. So what helps you, what provides you with a way to a closer relationship with God, is going to be different to other people, as we are each on our own journey, linked only by our faith in God, Father, Son and Holy Spirit.

There is no such thing as instant knowledge, or instant faith, listen to friends, try different ways to pray, read different books, but use what brings you closer to God. We began with the question 'Do I need to go to College?' The answer is the same as above, if you are the type of person who thrives on study and the challenges provided by exams, then yes go to college, but never think it will replace your prayer time. Equally if you aren't really that academic or have no time for college, there are on-line course which cost nothing and don't expect you to pass exams and allow you to work at your own speed, then try them out. No matter how great or how little your scholarly knowledge is God will always be there waiting for you to =come and be loved by Him.

Obstacles on the journey
Some travellers never make it to their
Destination, because they are unprepared for
Obstacles they encounter. Too often these
Obstacles leave pilgrims frustrated or
Disoriented, resigned to make little or no
Headway. Spiritual dryness, prayerlessness
Temptation and discouragement can make us
Wonder whether it is possible or worthwhile to
Stay the course of Christian pilgrimage.
John Newton, Origen, the Desert Fathers and
Evelyn Underhill measure us there is a way
Through these obstacles. More than that, these
Masters of the spiritual life invite us to
Understand that, approached rightly, these
Obstacles have potential to move us forward
On the hard but joyful road
Of Christian Pilgrimage. 57

DO I NEED TO DRESS LIKE A HIPPY OR WEAR ORANGE ROBES?

"Spirituality is the insignia of the New Age...But by definition it must be holistic, not exclusive. Thus yoga, crystals, mind linking, dance, massage, and every other conceivable kind of therapy have their place as part of the recovery of true 'spiritual technology'. The use of imagination is encourage in visualization, but there are danger for children in the vast array of fantasy games on sale, which encourage them to imagine 'spirit guides' for their journey or to identify with dark powers." [58]

How would you respond to a friend who has been

using what you consider 'not Christian' things to bring her closer to God, things which have made her prayer time so much more uplifting?

You can't say it's not Christian and she should stop immediately as this would alienate her, but would you be willing to listen to what she said and find out how much it has helped her?

Is spirituality one of those words which can be used by many different people to mean many different things?

We know from looking at various definition in chapter one, that it can be, but how can we therefore know what it is, and when it is or isn't Christian?

How can anyone know, or decide, about what is Christian, if it can be so many things to different people and different religions?

Do people who consider themselves Agnostic or Atheist have spirituality?

In the last chapter we looked at the link between theology and spirituality which brought us closer to God. We also looked at how different groups/communities had different rules of life and different emphasis on Jesus' life, death and resurrection. Their differences didn't make one better than the other, they simple provide different ways for individuals to live out their life in relationship with God.

Let's look at this from a different angle. In the Grove booklets spirituality section there is a booklet call, "Sculpture, prayer and Spirituality." People find using their five senses in their prayer gives them a new way of relating to God and to each other. Sculpture is not something which I would choose, but I do like drawing creation and I like walking.

Mindfulness is seeing an upsurge in interest, particularly in relation to colouring, and drawing etc. It helps people to relax, find their inner self where they can begin to relate to God and listen to Him.

Others find yoga or Tai Chi helpful to getting their bodies to a relaxed place where they can come to God and listen to Him.

Would you consider doing a prayer walk?

"Deliberately use each of your senses one by one. Turn what you see and hear, touch and smell into a prayer of praise, wonder, intercession and petition.

Then let your thoughts go where they will. Be a butterfly, flitting from topic to topic at random.

Find an object, a fallen leaf, a stone, a feather, even a discarded wrapper and take it home to remind you to go on praying about whatever was most preoccupying you on the walk." [59]

What about using a candle, music, icons, repeated phrases like the Jesus prayer or the Hail Mary? Some will look at the list and say, "that's a bit too Catholic for me", or "that's what high Church people do. I know people who would feel very uncomfortable at the idea of using incense or an icon, "that's alright for the Orthodox, but I'm a Christian!" I did point out to him that so were the Orthodox, but he still felt uncomfortable. Icons for some are idolatry. But this is misunderstanding on their part. If you speak to an Orthodox person about icons, they will explain that it is a windows or doorways to God. They are not worshipping the actual picture, but using it as a way to God. When the western Church split theology and spirituality, the Eastern Orthodox Church didn't. They have always maintained a link between learning and the lives they lead, and icons are a large part of their liturgy both in Church and at home.

For them, "Prayer is communion, fellowship, union with God. There are no techniques, methods, exercises or forms which can manipulate or coerce God. Prayer is not magic and methods are not magical formulae." [60]

They believe that prayer is not something we do, but is something we are. "Prayer is God – it is not something I initiate, but something which I share: it is not primarily something that I do, but something God is doing in me: as St Paul says, 'not I, but Christ in me', (Gal 2:20)" [61]

They make use of the Jesus prayer, not for vain repetition in order to keep one awake or to get rid of distractions, but a repetition of love, praise, worship and human need. In that one single phrase we find a summary of the Gospels: moment of adoration, moment of penitence. In the New Testament Jesus' name was used in healing and to remove demons.

"Consider it not as a prayer empties of thought, but as a prayer filled with the beloved." [62]

Going back to where we began, new age spirituality, below is a table comparing Christian spirituality and new age spirituality. Our prayer, liturgy, our whole focus is on God.

Christian	New Age
➢ Our gaze is always on the Glory of God. ➢ We aim to deepen our relationship of love. ➢ Jesus Christ is our Lord.	➢ Seeking a change of consciousness. ➢ Positive thinking. ➢ Inner directed meditation. ➢ Concerned with change both personal and individual.

This is just a brief description of the differences, but it gives us an idea of the type of discernment we need to use when reading or thinking about peoples suggestions to help us in our prayers. Saying this, many people adapt things from new age and other religions for a Christian use within their lives. One things we cannot do when people are trying to help us, or trying to explain what has helped them, is to say, "I don't do it that way, it's not the Anglican (any religion) way.

In turn someone could say, "What exactly is the Anglican way?" which is an even tougher question to answer. If you look at the Anglican/Church of England churches throughout the world, there is no one way. There are similarities in liturgy and spirituality is based on the Bible, plus the teaching of early Christians, monks, nuns and theologians through history, but the way people live, the emphasis on different things, their understanding varies from country to country, town to town, street to street.

There is a book called "Your God is to small" by JB Philips, it always reminds me of the modern phrase "thinking outside the box". So often in our lives we tend to put things in nice little boxes where we can easily control, understand and relate to things.

1Cor 13:11 "When I was a child, I talked like a child; I thought like a child, I reasoned like a child. When I became a man, I put the ways of childhood behind me."

Some of the points we disagree with others about may relate to the need to allow God out of the box to be the mysterious lovers who can't be controlled by us or any other part of His creation. So often God is something we get out on Sundays as we go to Church, but He is the creator, He is so much more than we can ever understand, but so often we try to limit Him to what we can understand. Our view of God should change as we grow and develop as Christians. In the first chapter I suggested you think about "How do I view God?" This is a serious question we all need to think about, if, as we discussed earlier, prayer and spirituality are about being with God, how can we do this if we still have ideas about God which date back to when we were ten?

Not only do we need to get God out of the box, we also need to be open to Him and open to try and find ways which you as one individual find helpful, to relate to Him, to listen to Him and to let Him love us. Spirituality is a variety of things to different people as we've seen in the last few chapters, but if we were to pick three words which seem to be common to all the different ideas we've looked at so far would be; God, love and You. No matter whether we are looking at Jesus' disciples or nuns and monks of the twenty-first century, the message is always, God loves you.

Sometimes it seems a lot easier to worry about this friend or that, trying to help them get going in prayer or listening when times get tough, but this is simply us trying to avoid our own relationship with God. We justify it as "sharing God's love", when in essence it is avoidance. We all need time with God, just as much as our friends and family do.

We have wandered slightly, but all for the good hopefully. New Age, other religions, yoga, tai chi all have a spirituality of their own, but equally we can learn from them ways which we can use in a Christian way. Our society is multi-cultural, and multi-faith, and many within society, both adults and children, are searching for something to fill a void in their lives. Some of this need is filled by drugs or alcohol; others try out different religions, while others may be lured by magic or some of the darker arts. They need to know about spirituality, but so often they don't have a good view of the Church, or they think it is just for older people. They need to see Christians out on the streets, sharing God's love, not necessarily by words, but by actions.

❖   How can the Church respond to the needs of

these people, when their ideas of the Church are fairly negative?

❖ How can you grow as a Christian living in a multi-cultural and multi-faith society?

❖ Macquarie says, "Prayer is at the heart of all religions, but for many Christians prayer has become something of an embarrassment." Do you think this is true of the people you know?[63]

> May God bless us,
>
> That in us may be found love and humility
>
> Obedience and thanksgiving,
>
> Discipline, gentleness and peace.
>
> Amen

DO I NEED
A GUIDE,
CONFESSOR OR
THERAPIST?

"The Priest is primarily concerned with spirituality as the fundamental requirement of health. The therapist or counsellor primarily concerned with sickness." [64]

In the twenty first century there are more therapists/counsellors helping Christians than there are spiritual directors. Through the previous centuries there was a need for spiritual directors or/and confessors, (could be the same person on occasions).

Thoughts:

- Do Priests consider themselves as counsellors as well as Parish Priests?
- Is pastoral care more than just therapeutic?
- Where does confession fall, is it part of pastoral care or is it more of a counsellors role?

There are Priests who are also trained as counsellors and therefore it aids there pastoral work, but the majority aren't trained, unless they choose to spend extra time training. This may be the time when the idea of preaching, teaching and healing were brought together, and this was originally what the disciples were sent out by Jesus to do. (Did we forget, or was it just all put together under pastoral care?)

Much of this began in the United States, but there has also been an increase in Britain. Is this where the idea of hospital and prison chaplains came about? There was a movement in the 1950's in Britain called Clinical Theology. This is also around the time that pastoral care and the cure of souls became a part of the Priests role.

So why did all this come about?

You can see examples of spiritual guides all the way back to the time of the Desert Fathers and Mothers. Often this was done by writing as well as by meeting people, now a days the majority of directors meet with people, although you can find people who communicate by facetime, skype, phone or email. I often wonder how the ones which happen by letter, text or email really work, because people often give away more through gestures and body language than by written communications.

Confession also goes back a long way. The Bible says that we are born in sin, which means there is a gulf between us and God, and therefore, as we are made in God's image, there is a gulf between who we think we are and who God created us to be.

Sin is any way of life, (actions, words or thoughts), that falls short of God's will and purpose for us. The power and significance of sin lies in a profound confusion about our true identity. The death and Resurrection of Christ therefore is a way in which a bridge is built between us and God, so you may ask, why do we need confession? But the better question is, why, after Jesus died and rose again for us, do we still fall into sin? Human nature? Confession therefore has a role within our lives both within the liturgy, at home in our prayers, and in a more specific way in the act of reconciliation.

> "Dear God,
> When we fall,
> Let us fall inwards;
> Let us fall freely and completely;
> That we may find our depth and humility:
> The solid earth from which
> We may rise up and love again." (By M. Leu-

ing) [65]

What views do you have on confession, with your parish priest or some other priest? "Many people outside the Catholic tradition tend to have a jaundiced view of confession". [66]

During the reformation they tried to rid the Church of all superstitions, they brought in the sale of indulgences and made regular confession essential for a person salvation. The problem today is that many think it's not very relevant to their lives, even some Catholics. When it comes up in conversation, most people will quickly move onto easier topics.

Yet there are many people for whom the whole idea of preparing and writing a list in preparation really helps, particularly with sins which have been haunting them for years or most of their lives. Despite the emphasis on modern psychotherapy and counselling, there is a slow resurgence, even with those of a non-Catholic tradition. Is this partly because there is an emphasis on confession as a form of reconciliation and an aid to spiritual growth? No one knows completely, but it is becoming more available and accepted. Along with rules of life, keeping journals and becoming friends of societies. These are seen of way people can reach out for help, guidance and a renewed sense of spirituality in their lives, which many are searching for.

A rule of life is nowhere as daunting as it sounds. It is something people living in communities have, guiding them about prayer, liturgy, work, food and social times.

Becoming a friend, associate or a tertiary (depending on the community you choose), will probably think about a rule for their lives. They live there normal lives, but are linked to a specific convent or monastery, praying for them , joining with them for some services during the year and maybe going on retreat with them.

When we speak of a rule of life for many it sounds rather formal and quite restrictive, but rule has a different meaning today. "Rule is the means by which, under God, we take responsibility for the pattern of our spiritual lives." [66] Rule means a path, a guide, a way of life, not constrictive, but giving freedom. Rather than "I should", or "I must", it is "I will try" or "With the help of God I will"......A rule brings a shape to your life and allows you to plan time at work, with family and with God.

Even now, without being aware of it we have a rule to our lives. We know when we get up, what order we do things, what time we leave the house, what time we eat, what time we get home and many other things, we just do it without thinking. (Even the television and the radio present you with a plan for the day, week, or month ahead.)

The most important thing about a rule is to make it manageable.

	Personal	Family	Friends	Work	Church	Leisure

Daily						
Weekly						
Monthly						
Yearly						

This is a very simple and straight forward plan, but you can create it in any way which you feel will help you. This is something private between you and God, no one else needs to know unless you choose to tell them. It isn't a way to score brownie points with God, just a way to expand your time with Him and with those around you.

People often also seek out a spiritual director, or a guide, to help them to understand things and to move forward in areas they may feel stuck. The idea began in communities where one of the older brothers/sisters would spend time, each week with the newer community members helping them to understand more about the life of the community. They are usually people who are mature in their faith and are open to listening and helping people to grow. There are many courses these people can go on, so they can learn more about helping others.

Thomas Merton says, "The spiritual director is concerned with the whole person, for the spiritual life is not just the life of the mind or of the affections, or of the 'summit of the soul' – it is the life of the whole person."[67]

So you are looking for someone you can trust, you can feel confident enough that he/she won't react to the things you have to share with them, someone who knows God intimately and has travelled away on their journey.

When we were talking about the rule of life, I mentioned retreats, this may or may not be something you've heard of or experienced before. Often Churches or groups have quiet days at a local community. These are days with two or three talks on a specific subject, time for thought and prayer and may finish with a communion service. These are like small retreats. People will go away for a weekend or a week and stay at a community, maybe near home, or further away. Sometimes these are fully silent, sometimes there are just certain times of silence during each day. Retreats can be for individuals or with a group who you may or may not know. It is a good way to get out of our 9 – 5 life and spend time with God and also with ourselves. Often our lives are so busy we have little time to relax and come to terms with the way our life is going. So a retreat is a good way to spend time with God thinking about the life you are living. It is not difficult, but I know the first time can feel slightly overwhelming; what do I do for the silence; can I read, or should I pray: do I need to kneel down or is sitting ok; if I have a question who do I ask and when do I ask; these and many other questions may pass through your mind as you sit in the chapel ready for the first talk. All I can suggest is begin small and begin with a guided retreat so you have someone to work through questions with.

Consider this story:

> "There were three brothers who lived with their father. After he had died, they wondered about their futures. The eldest brother said, "I'm off to give health to the world." The second brother said, "I'm off to spread education around the world." And the third brother said, "I'm staying here."
>
> A year or two passed and the eldest brother returned. He said, "I am exhausted and dis-eased." The second brother came home and said, "I am weary and confused." The third brother said, "Wait here. I'm going to fetch water from the river."
>
> He came back with a bowl full of water. It was thick and murky, but he asked his brothers to sit round it and silently watch it. Gradually the water settled and the mud fell to the bottom; the water became so clear the brothers could see their faces reflected in it. The peace and stillness enveloped them.
>
> "You see," said the youngest brother, "it is only when you are still enough to know your own faces that you can hear what God wants of you. Only then can you act in God's power." [68.]

How does all this fit in with our theme, "What is Spirituality?", if spirituality is about love, Gods of us and ours of God, then we need to find ways to bring us closer to God and to help us grow in our faith and understanding.

> Love bade me welcome yet my should drew back,
>> Guilty of dust and sin
>> But quick love, observing me grow slack,
>> From my first entrance,
>> Drew nearer to me, sweetly questioning
>> If I lacked anything.

> A guest, I answered , worthy to be free;
>> Have said. You shall be he,
>> I, the unkind, ungrateful? Ah my dear,
>> I cannot look on thee.
>> Love took my hand and smiling did reply
>> Who made the eye but I.

> Truth Word, but I have maimed them; let my shame,
>> Go where it doth deserve.
>> And know you not, says love, who bore the blame?
>> My dear then I will serve.
>> You must sit down says love, and taste my meat:
>> So I did sit and eat.

Love by George Herbert. 69.

AM I REALLY SPIRITUAL?

"He cannot be comprehended by our intellect, or any man's, or any angels for that matter. For both they and we are created beings. But only to our intellect is He incomprehensible, not to our love." [70]

"Your presence is in my life
Your presence is all around me
Your presence is peace.

Your presence is in my house,
Your presence is all around me,
Your presence is peace.

Your presence is in my work
Your presence is all around me
Your presence is peace." [71.]

All of God's creation is spiritual, whether or not people choose to acknowledge it and let it grow, like a small seed into a huge tree. Religion is not necessary as we've seen, nor is Christianity as there are many who would not consider themselves religious or Christian. But we have been focusing on Christian spirituality, so we look from the Bible through many prophets, monks, nuns, and many centuries to find a "definition". Although I'm not sure that's a good word to use as many have said, defining it is very difficult as it is a slippery word. Just as we cannot define God, for defining Him means putting in a box which then limits Him and limits our relationship with Him.

Spirituality, like Vocation is words which are about God, His creation and about us. It's about why God created everything we see around us, and much more we can't see, but especially about why He created us. He created us in His images. So we could be one with Him, so that He could love us and we could love Him, and then go out and share His love with all we meet.

You may ask why would He choose to love me, I have done so much wrong; I even find it hard to love myself?

Things happen which we regret, things happen which have us feeling ashamed but despite all this, God created us to be loved by Him and for us to love Him and ourselves. We cannot truly love God, if we don't love ourselves as we are part of His creation and a part of God, and made in His image. He sent His own Son to die for us, so that we could relate to Him, that's how much He loves us.

How do we come to know God? Through the Bible,

through the liturgy, through Church, through books we read, through friends and family and through our own private prayer where we talk to Him and listen to what He has to say.

Spirituality is about a way of life, a way of love and a way of being whole.

I'm not sure if anything here has changed your way of thinking or living, but I left this simple exercise for the end, which you can use now or when you feel its right.

North Window

East Window

West window

South Window

"Exploring the windows of your life:

East window is what is rising above the horizon for you.

West window is what is dying off in your life and sinking below the horizon.

North window is what holds you steady, keeps you doming from or pointing to.

South window is warming the creativity of your life." [72]

FOOTNOTES:

1. Discover your Spirituality. J. Hinton pg 5
2. Ibid, pg 5
3. Ibid, pg 7
4. Signposts to Spirituality, T. Hudson. Pg 15
5. Spirituality and Pastoral Care. K. Leech Pg 7
6. Spirituality and Theology. P. Sheldrake. Pg 57.
7. Beyond Boundaries. J. Robinson. Pg 64
8. The Spiritual Workbook. D. Runcorn. Pg 325.
9. The Study of Spirituality. Ed. Jones Wainright & Yarnold. Pg xxvi
10. Ibid Pg 538
11. Wisdom Distilled. J. Chittister. Pg 4
12. Signposts to Spirituality. T. Hudson. Pg 19
13. Ibid, pg 22
14. Spirituality and Pastoral Care. K. Leech. Pg 9
15. Ibid, pg 9
16. The Spiritual Workbook. D. Runcorn. Pg 120
17. Ibid, pg 122
18. Spirituality and Pastoral Care. K. Leech. Pg

9

19. The Desert of the Heart. Ed. Sr Benedicta. Ward. SLG pg x
20. Ibid. pg xi
21. The Cry of the Deer. D. Adams. Pg 7
22. The Study of Spirituality. Ed Jones, Wainwright & Yarwuld. Pg 9
23. Ibid. pg 36
24. Ibid. pg 565
25. Paths in Spirituality. J. Macquarrie. Pg 28.
26. Spirituality and Pastoral Care. K. Leech. Pg 31
27. When I awake. J. Winslow. Pg 9
28. Personality and Prayer. R. Folke.. Pg viii
29. Ibid. pg vii
30. Ibid. pg 5
31. The Spirituality of St Patrick. L. Whiteside. Pg 23
32. Ibid. pg 10
33. Ibid. pg 21
34. Ibid. pg 12
35. Augustine and the Journey to Wholeness. R. Innes. Pg 4
36. Wisdom Distilled. J. Chittister OSB. Pg 7
37. Ibid. pg 15
38. Anselm of Canterbury. Sr Benedicta Ward SLF. Pg 11
39. Ibid. pg 11
40. Psalm 46:16
41. Spirituality and Pastoral Care. K. Leech. Pg 20

42. The Cry of the Deer. D. Adams. Pg 100
43. Spirituality and Theology. P. Sheldrake. Pg xi
44. Ibid. pg 36
45. Ibid. pg 3
46. Ibid. pg 16
47. Who was Julian? M. McLean. Pg 1
48. Ibid. pg 13
49. Ibid. pg 15
50. Ibid. pg 16
51. Praying in the Franciscan Spirit. Pg 6
52. Wikipedia, Apophatic Theology.
53. The Intimacy you Desire. T. Elliot. Pg 9.
54. The Fountain and the Furnace. M. Ross. Pg 272
55. Personality and Prayer. R. Folke. Pg. 45
56. The Fountain and the Furnace. M. Ross pg 278
57. Companions for your Spiritual Journey. M. Harris. Pg 53.
58. Grove Spirituality Series. No. 34. Pg 12
59. Personality and Prayer. R. Folke. Pg 36.
60. Spiritual Workbook. D. Runcorn. Pg 11
61. The Power of the name. K. Ware. Pg 8
62. Ibid. pg 23
63. Paths in Spirituality. J. Macquarrie. Pg 25
64. Soul Friend. K. Leech. Pg 101
65. Spiritual Workbook. D. Runcorn. .pg 129
66. Grove Spirituality Series, No 92. Pg 4
67. Grove Spirituality Series. No. 9. Pg 7
68. Grove Spirituality Series. No. 92. Pg 4

69. The Fountain and the Furnace. M. Ross. Pg 127

70. The Cry of the Deer. D. Adams. Pg 100

71. Ibid. pg 18-19

72. Spiritual Workbook. D. Runcorn Pg 117

BIBLIOGRAPHY:

Adams. D. The Cry of the Deer.
Triangle/SPCK, London, 1987.

Barry. W. Spiritual Direction and the Encounter with God.
Paulist Press, New Jersey, 2004.

Brother Ramon. Praying the Jesus Prayer.
Marshall Publishing, Basingstoke, 1988

Chittister. J. Wisdom Distilled from the Daily.
Harper Collins, San Francisco, 1990.

Elliot. T. The Intimacy you Desire.
Twenty-third publications, New London, 2018.

Folke. R. Personality and Prayer.
Eagle, Surrey, 1999.

Foster. R. Spiritual Formation Workbook.
Harper Collins Publishers, London, 1993.

Harris. M. Companions for your Spiritual Journey.
Intervarsity Press, Surrey, 1999.

Hinton. J. Discover your Spirituality.

Hunt & Thorpe. Australia, 1992.

Hollingburt, Richmond, Whitcheat. Equipping your Church in a Spiritual age.
Group for Evangelism, Sheffield, 1990.

Hudson. D. Signposts to Spirituality.
Stoke Christian Books, Michigan, 1995.

Johnson. R. Your Personality and the Spiritual Life.
Lion Hudson PLC, USA, 1995.

Kelly. F. Praying in the Celtic Spirit.
Kevin Mayhew, Suffolk, 1999.

Leech. K. Spirituality and Pastoral Care.
Sheldon Press, London, 1986

Leech. K. Soul Friend.
Sheldon Press, London, 1977

Leech. K. True God.
Sheldon Press, London, 1997

McLean. Who was Julian?
Julian Shrine Publications, Norwich, 1984.

McGeal. (O.Carm.) Praying the Carmelite Spirit.
Kevin Mayhew, Suffolk, 1998.

Macquarrie. J. Paths in Spirituality.
SCM Press Ltd, London, 1972.

O'Mahoney. G. SJ. Praying in the Ignatian Spirit.
Kevin Mayhew, Suffolk, 1998.

Robinson. J. Beyond Boundaries.
Libertas Publishing, UK, 2017

Runcorn. D. Spiritual Workbook.
SPCK, London, 2006.

Sheldrake. P. Spirituality and Theology.
Dartman, Longman & Todd Ltd, London, 1998

Sr. Benedicta Ward, SLG. Anselm of Canterbury.
SLG Press, Oxford, 1973.

Sr. Francis Teresa OSG. Praying in the Franciscan Spirit.
Kevin Mayhew, Suffolk, 1999.

Ware. K. The Power of the Name.
Marshall Pickering, London, 1989.

Winslow. J. When I awake.
Hodder & Stoughton Ltd, Suffolk, 1938.
****

Ed. Blackhouse. H. The Cloud of Unknowing.
Hodder and Stoughton, London, 1985.

Ed. Johnson, Wainwright, Yarwauld. The Study of Spirituality.
SPCK, London, 1986.

Ed. Sr Benedicta Ward SLG. The Desert of the Heart.
Darton, Longman & Todd, London, 1988.

****

Grove Spirituality Series.

Grove Books Ltd, Cambridge.

No 8 – Finding a Personal Rule. 1984

No 15 – Dreams and Spirituality, 1985.

No 29 – Advance by Retreat. 1988.

No 32 – Meeting God in Creation. 1990.

No 50 – Personal Confession Reconsidered. 1994.

No 65 – An Introduction to the Imitation of Christ. 1998.

No 68 – Learning from English Mystics. 1999.

No 88 – Augustine and his Journey to Wholeness. 2004.

No 92 - Simple tools for Silence. 2005.

Printed in Great Britain
by Amazon